My Little Christmas Book
THE NUTCRACKER

NEW SEASONS

PUBLISHING

Copyright © 1996 Publications International, Ltd.
ISBN 0-7853-2075-X
Contributing writer: Carolyn Quattrocki
Illustrations: Susan Spellman

It was Christmas Eve—at last! Marie and her brother Fritz could not remember such a wonderful celebration. After dinner, they opened presents with their young cousins and friends. There were dolls, toy soldiers, and picture books for everyone. Marie's favorite gift was from her godfather, Dr. Drosselmeier. It was a wooden nutcracker carved to look like an old soldier.

The children played and danced, and they shared all kinds of Christmas candies and cookies. Then Dr. Drosselmeier said, "Wait right here, children. I have a special Christmas treat." He returned in a moment with two puppets and a small stage. The dolls leaped and twirled as if they were alive, while the children laughed and clapped. Marie held her nutcracker through the whole show.

After the show was over, Fritz began to dance around just like the puppets had done. He grabbed the nutcracker from Marie and leaped up high. But Fritz could not dance quite as well as the puppets. He stumbled, and the nutcracker went flying across the room.

When Marie ran to pick up her favorite gift, she saw that his wooden jaw was broken. "Oh, no!" she cried. "Let me fix you, poor nutcracker." She wrapped the nutcracker's jaw with her handkerchief and gently set him under the Christmas tree.

Then Mother called, "It's time for bed." All the guests had left, and it was time to put out the lights and go upstairs.

The house was quiet, but Marie could not sleep. She was thinking about the nutcracker under the Christmas tree.

Marie tiptoed downstairs. When she opened the doors to the big parlor, she was surprised to see that the Christmas tree was lighted again. She picked up her nutcracker, but he looked larger than when she had left him under the tree. And his jaw was not broken anymore!

The nutcracker also seemed to be growing taller, and his carved wooden face slowly changed. Before Marie's very eyes, he became a handsome young prince. The Prince bowed down low to Marie and thanked her. Her act of kindness had broken a magic spell that had been cast over him.

Marie heard squeaky, scuffly, scratchy sounds. She looked up to see a roomful of huge, gray mice. "What are mice doing here!" thought Marie. The mice were led by a Mouse King, who had seven heads and carried a sword.

Fritz's soldiers magically grew to life size and came to help the Prince. A great battle began, with the mice fighting the soldiers and the Mouse King fighting the Prince.

Marie feared that the mice would win. The Prince and the toy soldiers seemed to be getting tired. But she saw a chance to help. She took off her slipper and threw it with all her might at the Mouse King. Down he went! The battle was over, and the gray mice scurried away.

The Prince was now completely free from the magic spell. He could go home to his own land. "Would you come with me?" he asked Marie.

"Oh, yes!" she said.

The Prince led Marie to the Christmas tree and raised his arms. Suddenly they found themselves in the Prince's own kingdom, surrounded by beautiful, dancing snow fairies.

"Welcome to the Land of Sweets," said the Prince. Marie saw sights she had never dreamed of. Here, the houses were made of chocolate and peppermint sticks. There was a lake of sugar and almond milk and a sparkling river of lemonade with lollipop trees and candy flowers all along its banks. Marie and the Prince traveled down the lemonade river in a tiny seashell boat.

Finally, they arrived at a sparkling castle made entirely out of spun sugar. This was the palace of the Sugar Plum Fairy, who came out to meet them.

The Prince said, "Marie, with her kindness, has rescued me from an enchanted spell. In the battle with the Mouse King, at just the right moment, she threw her slipper and saved me."

When the Sugar Plum Fairy heard this, she invited Marie and the Prince to sit on her royal throne. She had a great party to celebrate. Everyone in the Land of Sweets came! As tinkling music filled the hall, the Sugar Plum Fairy did a graceful fairy dance. Next came a parade of dancers—Chinese dancers, whirling Arabian dancers, leaping and twirling Russian dancers.

Marie had never seen such sights! There were chocolate dancers and candy dancers and even dancing clowns. Just when Marie could not imagine anything more grand, she was surrounded by enchanted flowers.

Everywhere she looked were beautiful flowers—buttercups and daffodils, roses and tulips. They seemed almost to float as they waltzed round and round the great ballroom.

Everyone joined in the dancing. Marie was a little afraid to dance. Then the Nutcracker Prince came to her and said, "All this dancing is for you. You must dance, too. Come with me." So Marie and the Prince whirled and whirled and whirled . . .

. . . until Marie was a little dizzy and could no longer tell exactly where she was. She rubbed her eyes and sat up. She was beneath her own Christmas tree! In her own house. And here beside her was her nutcracker.

Where was the Prince? the dancers? the Sugar Plum Fairy? Oh, could it all have been a dream?